Harriet's
Had Enough!

Harriet's
Had Enough!

Elissa Haden Guest   illustrated by Paul Meisel

CANDLEWICK PRESS

One day Harriet and her mama had a big fight.
"Harriet, you need to clean up this mess," said Mama.
"What mess?" asked Harriet.
"*This* mess," said Mama. "This living room is a disaster!"
But Harriet kept on playing.

"Come on, now—let's pick up your toys," said Mama.

"Go away—I'm busy!" said Harriet.

"Harriet, you're being rude," said Mama. "It's time to clean up."

"I don't feel like it!" said Harriet. And she kicked over her blocks.

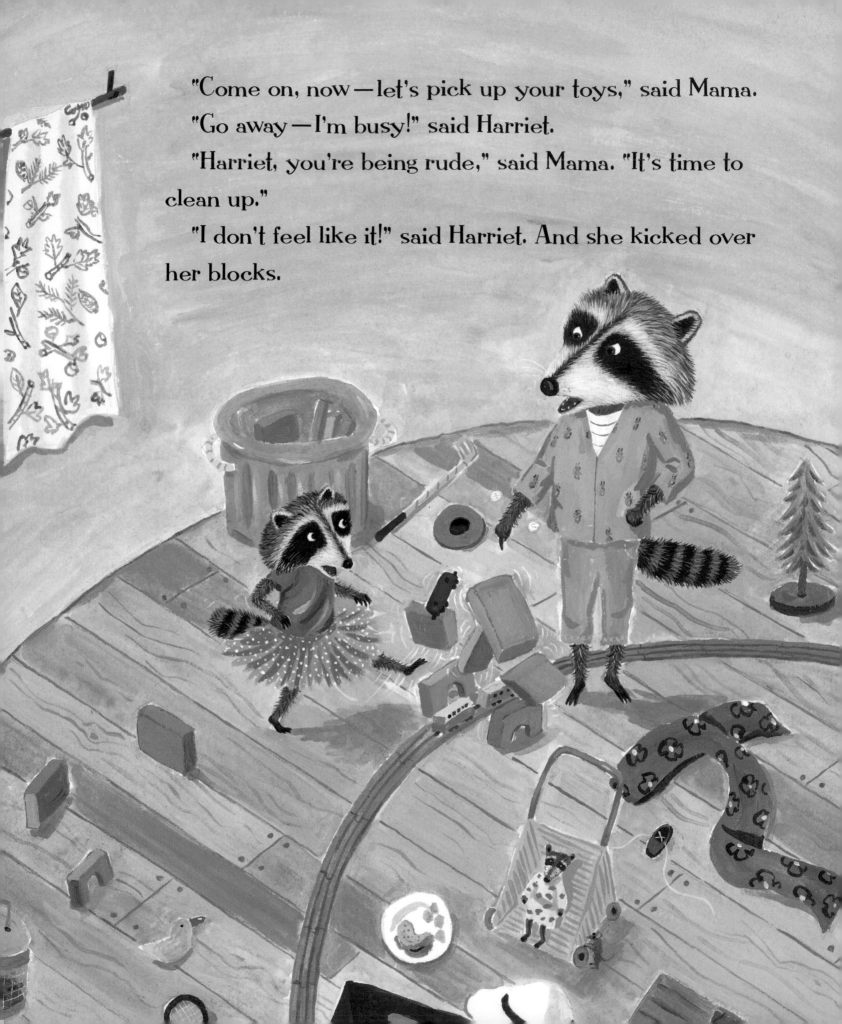

Mama picked up Harriet and carried her upstairs.
"You need to cool down," she said.
"YOU need to cool down!" said Harriet.

"Harriet, I'm fed up!" Mama shouted,
and she walked out of the room and
closed the door hard behind her.

"I'm fed up, too!" said Harriet. And she packed her suitcase and snapped it shut.

She was just about to leave when she heard Grandma call her name. Harriet peered out her window.

"Harriet, come look at these divine roses!" shouted Grandma.

Harriet picked up her suitcase and stomped downstairs and out into the garden.

"Where are you going, honey-bun?" asked Grandma.

"I'm running away!" said Harriet.

"All by your lonesome?" asked Grandma. "But why?"

"Because," said Harriet, "Mama's mean."

"What did she do?" asked Grandma.

"She yelled at me and said I had to clean up my toys!" said Harriet.

"Well, I have to clean up these weeds," said Grandma. "That's life, honey-bun."

"I'm still running away!" said Harriet.

"Oh, dear," said Grandma. "Promise you'll write to me every day?"

"Oh, all right!" said Harriet.

Harriet's grandma kissed Harriet all over her face and twice on her nose.

"Good-bye, Grandma," said Harriet.

Harriet picked up her suitcase and lugged it into the kitchen to find Papa.

"Where are you going, cookie?" asked Papa.

"I'm running away!" said Harriet.

"All by your lonesome?" asked Papa. "Why?"

"Because," said Harriet, "Mama's mean."

"What did she do?"

"She yelled and yelled at me and said I had to clean up my toys!" said Harriet.

"Well, I have to clean up these pots and pans," said Papa. "That's life, cookie."

"I'm still running away!" said Harriet.

"Before you go, would you mind tasting the spaghetti sauce?" Papa's tomato sauce was Harriet's favorite.

"Oh, all right!" said Harriet. Papa dipped the big wooden spoon into the simmering sauce. He blew on the spoon three times to cool it down. Harriet took a tiny sip. She closed her eyes and sighed.

"How is it?" asked Papa.

"Mm-mm. Divine," said Harriet.

"Sure you don't want to stay for dinner?"

Harriet smelled garlic bread baking in the oven. Her stomach rumbled.

"I can't. I'm running away!" said Harriet.

"Promise you'll call me every day and twice on Sundays?" asked Papa.

"OK," said Harriet.

Papa gave Harriet a big hug and patted her head.

Then Harriet picked up her suitcase and heaved it over to the front door.

"Good-bye, Papa," she said.

Harriet pushed the door open and stepped onto the front porch. And there—as if she were waiting—was Mama.

"Where are you going, honey?" she asked.

"I'm running away!" said Harriet. But her suitcase felt as heavy as stone.

"Let's talk," said Mama. Harriet shook her head no.

The sun was setting. Soon it would be dark.

"It's getting chilly," said Mama, and she slipped off her sweater and wrapped it around Harriet's shoulders like a cape. "How's that? Better?" Harriet nodded. Mama's sweater was cozy and warm.

"I hate when we fight," said Mama. "It makes me feel so . . ."

"Lonesome?" whispered Harriet.

"Yes," said Mama. "Come here, sweetheart, let's turn this day around." Harriet looked at Mama, then out at the darkening path.

Then she put down her suitcase for good
and flew into her mother's arms.

Harriet told Mama that she was sorry for not cleaning up.

"And for shouting and being rude?" asked Mama.

"That too," said Harriet.

And Mama said she was sorry for yelling at Harriet.

"And for slamming the door?" asked Harriet.

"That too," said Mama.

And then Papa came outside and said come to think
of it, he could use some help setting the table.

And Grandma came round and said she could use
some help making the bouquet.

And Harriet said she sure could use some help
cleaning up her toys.

So everyone pitched in and helped one another.

Then they all sat down to spaghetti dinner.

"Mm-mm. That was divine," said Harriet.

To my divine family —
Nick, Gena, and Nathanael — with love
E. H. G.

For Bryan, Olivia, Kathleen, and Bob Taylor
P. M.

Text copyright © 2009 by Elissa Haden Guest
Illustrations copyright © 2009 by Paul Meisel

First edition 2009

Library of Congress Cataloging-in-Publication Data

Guest, Elissa Haden.
Harriet's had enough! / Elissa Haden Guest ; illustrated by Paul Meisel. —1st ed.
p. cm.

Summary: Harriet and her mother exchange mean words when Harriet refuses to pick up her toys,
until an apology saves the day and everyone sits down to a spaghetti dinner.
ISBN 978-0-7636-3454-4

[1. Orderliness—Fiction. 2. Cleanliness—Fiction. 3. Behavior—Fiction. 4. Family life—Fiction.]
I. Meisel, Paul, ill. II. Title.
PZ7.G9375Ru 2009
[E]—dc22   2008019059

2 4 6 8 10 9 7 5 3 1

Printed in China

This book was typeset in Malonia Voigo.
The illustrations were done in watercolor, acrylic, and gouache on paper.

Candlewick Press
99 Dover Street
Somerville, Massachusetts 02144

visit us at www.candlewick.com